DREAM-ALONG

NURSERY RHYMES

Rookie
Nursery
Rhymes™

Children's Press®
An Imprint of Scholastic Inc.

Scholastic Inc., 557 Broadway, New York, NY 10012.

Library of Congress Cataloging-in-Publication Data

Names: Huliska-Beith, Laura, 1964- illustrator. | Reid, Mick, 1958- illustrator. | Allyn, Virginia, illustrator.
Title: Dream-along nursery rhymes.
Description: New York, NY : Children's Press, an imprint of Scholastic Inc.,
[2017] | Summary: Includes three traditional nursery rhymes,
illustrated by different people.
Identifiers: LCCN 2016005495| ISBN 9780531228777 (library binding) | ISBN 9780531229637 (pbk.)
Subjects: LCSH: Nursery rhymes. | Children's poetry. | CYAC: Nursery rhymes.
Classification: LCC PZ8.3 .D778 2017 | DDC 398.8—dc23 LC record available at http://lccn.loc.gov/2016005495

No part of this publication may be reproduced in whole or in part, or stored in a retrieval system, or transmitted in any form or
by any means, electronic, mechanical, photocopying, recording, or otherwise, without written permission of the publisher.
For information regarding permission, write to Scholastic Inc.,
Attention: Permissions Department, 557 Broadway, New York, NY 10012.

Produced by Spooky Cheetah Press
Design by Book & Look

© 2017 by Scholastic Inc.
All rights reserved. Published in 2017 by Children's Press, an imprint of Scholastic Inc.

Printed in China 62

SCHOLASTIC, CHILDREN'S PRESS, ROOKIE NURSERY RHYMES™, and associated logos
are trademarks and/or registered trademarks of Scholastic Inc.

4 5 6 7 8 9 10 R 25 24 23 22 21 20 19

Illustrations by Laura Huliska-Beith (LIttle Jack Horner), Mick Reid (Hey, Diddle, Diddle),
Virginia Allyn (There Was an Old Woman), and pp 6–12, 14–20, 22–28 (wooden bar) Venimo/Shutterstock

TABLE OF CONTENTS

LITTLE JACK HORNER

Illustrated by Laura Huliska-Beith

Listen to the audio here:

http://www.scholastic.com/NR4

Little Jack Horner

sat in the corner

eating his Christmas pie.

He stuck in his thumb

and he pulled out a plum.

And he said...

"What a good boy am I!"

HEY, DIDDLE, DIDDLE

Illustrated by Mick Reid

Listen to the
audio here:

http://www.scholastic.com/NR5

Hey, diddle, diddle,

the cat and the fiddle,

the cow jumped

over the moon.

The little dog laughed

to see such a sight,

and the dish ran away
with the spoon.

THERE WAS AN OLD WOMAN

Illustrated by Virginia Allyn

Listen to the audio here:

http://www.scholastic.com/NR6

There was an old woman

who lived in a shoe.

She had so many children,

she didn't know what to do.

So she gave them some broth

and plenty of bread.

Then she kissed them sweetly
and put them to bed.

Lots of animal friends are watching through the window as Jack eats his Christmas pie.

Take another look through the book.

- Count how many animals come to the window altogether. Can you name them all?

- Which animal peeked in the window first? Which one came last?

FUN WITH Hey, Diddle, Diddle
Pages 13 to 20

Doesn't this story sound like a funny dream?

Imagine other things that might have happened in the dream.

• The dog dances on the cow.
What other funny tricks might the dog do?

• The cow jumped over the moon.
    What other things
    might the cow jump over?

FUN WITH

There Was
an Old Woman
Pages 21 to 28

The old woman who lives
in a shoe has so many children!

Go back and count:

- How many of her children eat broth?
- How many of her children eat bread?
- How many children are in the
bunks, ready to go to bed?